The Fairies of
Waterfall Island

The Search for the Missing Crystal

Emma Sumner

You can do anything you put your mind to!

~ Emma

Two Free Gifts!

Before you start the book I have something special to share with you.

Gift #1

Get the free Audio Book of "The Fairies of Waterfall Island: The Search for the Missing Crystal" just by going to:

www.EmmaLovesBooks.com/audiobook

Gift #2

Download a free coloring sheet of one the main characters by going to:

www.EmmaLovesBooks.com/download

Thank you so much for purchasing this book, I hope that you will love it as much as I do. ☺

Table of Contents

Chapter 1
A Helpful Hand

"Hailey! Come quick! We have a problem!" shouted Mia as she flew along the white sand near the edge of Stargazers Cove. She was flying so fast that she almost didn't see the blonde-haired fairy hovering behind a pineapple on the beach below.

Mia, the oldest of four fairy sisters living on Waterfall Island, had beautiful black hair and a bright green dress that shimmered in the sun as she flew, but her long black hair was in a mess after flying so fast, and her wings were starting to curve down from their normal point because she was tired. "There you are!" she yelled to Hailey as she was trying to catch her breath, "You have to come with me back to the ocean just on the other side of Stargazers Cove. There is a dolphin that has washed up on shore. She is caught in a net, and Makenna needs our help to free her!"

Hailey stepped out from behind the pineapple and shouted, "Slow down, Mia! I can't understand you. What is going on?"

Hailey had been studying the seashells around her, looking up their names in her books. She was studying the animals in the area for fun because she loved to learn about any topic. Her blonde hair was pulled back behind her ears. She kept it shorter than all the other fairies in Sunset Village, so she could spend less time fixing her hair and more time reading. She had taught herself to read and write because there were no schools on the islands of the Crystal Kingdom.

After Mia repeated herself, Hailey started to worry. She knew that Makenna rarely needed any help with animals because out of all the fairies on Waterfall Island, their sister Makenna was the animal expert of the group.

"If Makenna needs our help with animals, this must be a big problem," noted Hailey. "Let's go!"

The two fairies rushed to help their sister. As they arrived, Makenna was waving her wand up and down quickly. When she saw the two fairies arrive, she shouted, "Thank goodness you are here. I need your help. This is a big problem!"

The fairies looked down at the young dolphin. It was screeching as it lay in the sand, stuck in a fisherman's net.

Makenna's wavy brown hair was pulled back with a blue headband keeping it from getting in her face. She had beautiful green eyes with a long, layered dress that was designed to look like blue leaves.

She loved to help animals that were in trouble and even had a pet fish that she visited each morning in the beach. The fish had pearly white scales that looked like sequins when it was in the sun.

Makenna told them that when she arrived at the beach that morning, she saw the dolphin caught in a fisherman's net. She did not know how the fisherman's net had gotten there, but she was determined to help the dolphin.

Makenna had been trying for hours since the sun came up to cut away the nets, but they were just too big and tangled for her to cut through. When the sun started to get hotter and she saw the dolphin getting weaker, she decided it was time to use her magic to free the dolphin. However, every time she lifted her wand, her magic faded away and the net remained in place—and time was running out for the dolphin.

"I don't understand," said Hailey, "How can your magic be fading away? We just got pixie dust two days ago?"

"I'm not sure either," admitted Mia. "Maybe we could use our wands together and set the dolphin free?"

The three fairies worked together using all their powers combined, and the fisherman's net slowly faded away. Strangely, even when they'd combined their magic, it took much more effort than it should have to free the dolphin. The fairies were surprised that their magic seemed to be weaker on that day.

Nevertheless, they had succeeded in freeing the dolphin. When she started to swim around, the dolphin was still a little shocked from the net. Eventually she started to swim faster and faster in delight and raised her body up in the air, just swimming on her tail, waving her fins to say thank you, and swam away to find her mother.

As the dolphin departed, the three fairies heard a small screeching sound. At first they thought it was the dolphin, but as the sound got louder, they realized it was their youngest sister, Rosey. With her light brown hair flowing behind her against her blue dress, Rosey always kept a flower behind her ear. Today the flower was bright yellow and shining like the sun, so it was easy for her sisters to see her coming.

Rosey always panicked over little things, but this time it wasn't that little. It was the most important ceremony of the year!

Chapter 2

You Panic Too Much

As Rosey was flying toward her sisters, they all looked at each other. Hailey whispered, "What is she screaming about this time?"

In a high-pitched voice, Rosey kept repeating, "We're gonna be late for the ceremony! We're gonna be late for the ceremony!"

The fairies looked at each other. Then they laughed. "The ceremony doesn't start for two hours," explained Mia. Mia, always the calmest and bravest of the sisters, knew that Rosey was panicking too much.

Rosey did not slow down. Instead, she just flew faster and anxiously voiced, "I know, but two hours is not enough time. We're gonna be late, we're gonna be late!"

Mia, Makenna, and Hailey quickly decided that they would get going—that way Rosey would stop panicking.

The fairies started back along the path home. On the way, Rosey was flying so fast, that the other fairies couldn't keep up.

From the beach they followed the path that led them home. They flew over Starlight Stream and past Seashell Bridge to their small but cozy home at the edge of Breeze Street in Sunset Village.

When they came in the door, the three older fairy sisters looked at each other in shock—Rosey already had their dresses prepared and laid out on each of their beds.

Each dress was a beautiful blue that started at the top with a deep dark blue that faded lighter and lighter until it was white at the bottom. The dresses were cut asymmetrically, angling toward the left side with one strap at the top on the right shoulder. All the dresses looked exactly the same with white roses running from the single strap on the right all the way to the area near the left shoulder.

It was the traditional dress of the Crystal Ceremony. This year's Crystal Ceremony was held to honor the Water Crystal and the gift of magic that the Water Crystal brought to the fairies of Waterfall Island.

Each island in Crystal Kingdom had been blessed with a crystal that was the source of magic and fairy dust. Without the crystal, no magic was possible in the fairy world. There were five crystals in total, one for each of the

Fairy Islands: the Water Crystal, the Fire Crystal, the Ice Crystal, the Flower Crystal, and the Rainbow Crystal. The Water Crystal, of course, was given to Waterfall Island. It was a sky blue but was not meant for the sky.

The crystals were kept in Crystal Palace where the king and queen lived. Crystal Palace sat in the middle of all the Fairy Islands and connected to each island by magic bridges. The crystals were kept safe there by a magical spell that only allowed the royal family to cross the bridges. The king and queen rarely left the castle because they were keeping guard of the crystals.

The ceremony to honor the Water Crystal was held every four years, and it was considered an honor to be chosen to perform at the ceremony—an honor that had been given to the four sisters Mia, Hailey, Makenna, and Rosey. No wonder Rosey was anxious and excited!

Chapter 3
Fireworks and Dancing

The four fairies were gathered behind the stage with their dresses on. They had the honor of dancing first in the ceremony.

Even though they had been practicing for weeks, Rosey was still worried that she was going to forget everything. She had even been practicing at home in secret, after the others had stopped for the day, and knew the dance better than anyone else, but that did not help calm her nerves.

Julia, the wisest fairy in Waterfall Island and the host of the ceremony, welcomed and thanked everyone for coming, and introduced the dancers. Julia had been to every ceremony for the last twenty years, even the ones for the other islands, and knew more about the crystals than any of the other fairies, except the king or queen.

With a little bit of music and a large burst of fireworks, Julia started the ceremony. The dance floor was a shallow pond of water, and the fairies glided across it to make beautiful patterns in the pond.

In the middle of the four sisters' opening dance, the water in the pond started slowly fading away. The music stopped, and a hush fell over the crowd. Julia tried to use her magic to restore the water in the pond, but each time she tried, nothing happened. Nobody could believe what was happening—after all, Julia was the strongest fairy in Waterfall Island. In fact, she was the fourth most powerful fairy in the entire kingdom.

"Oh no, this can't be," whispered Julia softly. After taking a minute to think, she realized she still had a little bit of power left. Additionally she determined there must be something wrong with the Water Crystal. She had a bad feeling that if something were wrong with one crystal, then something might be wrong with all the crystals.

Julie did not have the power to see exactly what was wrong, but she did have the ability to look into the future. So, she focused all her strength and used it to look into the future. Julia saw a group of four fairy sisters traveling with two humans, a boy and a girl. The humans were small and seemed to be children still. She saw them going on a great adventure together. At last, she saw the most surprising thing of all: Rosey, the most timid and scared fairy in all of Waterfall Island, saving everyone.

Before Julia could see more, the magic faded away.

The fairy sisters, Mia, Hailey, Makenna, and Rosey, flew toward Julia. They could see that she was sad and desperate, and they wanted to help.

Mia, having arrived first, asked, "What's wrong?"

"There is something wrong with the Water Crystal, and I fear all the other crystals as well. You four have been chosen to save our home, with the help of two humans, a boy and a girl," shared Julia.

Then she stepped toward Rosey.

Rosey stepped back, scared and wanting to hide behind her sisters.

Julia spoke directly to Rosey, "You will be the one to save Waterfall Island."

Rosey was afraid to move. She felt there had to be some mistake. Even she knew she was the biggest scaredy cat of all the sisters. She was not proud of it, but she could not help it. She dreamed of being as brave as Mia and wished that what Julia said could somehow be true, but she knew in her heart there must be some mistake.

Chapter 4
Reading Is Fun

After the ceremony was cancelled, the four fairies went home and gathered in Mia's room around her bed to discuss what Julia had said. "How are we going to get the help of humans?" questioned Makenna.

Hailey spoke up, "I have a book that can show us how to get the human world. I don't know if it is true, but it is worth a shot."

They followed Hailey out of the house and into her library. She had built a small building outside their tiny home because her room was not big enough to hold all her books. Once inside, Hailey headed to a shelf that had more than a dozen books on it. She grabbed a brown, dusty book and shouted, "Here it is!"

The book's title was *All About Humans*, and it had small papers stuffed in various places in it where Hailey had made notes. In the last section of the book, Hailey found what she was looking for, the chapter "How to Get There" that had specific directions on how to get to the human world.

The book told the sisters about a magic portal in the oldest tree on Waterfall Island. Makenna interrupted, yelling, "I know where it is, right next to the museum!" The book said that there would be a hollow in the tree, and if anyone went through it, there would be a portal to the human world.

After the fairies read the book, Hailey asked, "How will we know which humans will help us?"

Then Mia reminded her, "You know what Julia always says, let the magic come to you."

The four fairies flew to the museum to find the tree. Rosey started fast, flying along with her sisters, but then got slower and slower as she went. She was scared and didn't know whether she would have the courage to continue.

Once they arrived at the tree, the sisters saw the hollow part and knew that it must be the portal. Mia was the first to go in, followed by Makenna, then Hailey, and—because Rosey would rather be with her sisters than be home alone—finally Rosey went in too.

Chapter 5

A Portal So Powerful

When the fairies emerged on the other side of the portal, they found themselves standing in the yard of the biggest house they had ever seen. Rosey started to scream and hid behind Mia.

Makenna was the first one to speak, saying quietly, "This must be where the humans live."

Walking toward the house was a young girl. The fairies flew up to her and landed on her hand. The papers in her hand showed that her name was Kaylia.

When Kaylia noticed the fairies, at first she thought that she was dreaming, but then she realized that it was real.

"Oh my gosh!" screamed Kaylia in excitement. "Jack, come here!"

A young boy came running up. "What?" inquired Jack with a sigh, looking like he just got out of bed.

"Fairies! On my hand!" exclaimed Kaylia.

Jack, looking at her like she was crazy, murmured, "There is no such thing as . . ." Then he saw what was on Kaylia's hand and gasped, "Oh my gosh, there are fairies!"

Then they heard a small voice come from one of the fairies. "Yes, calm down," said Mia gently, "We have come for help. Will you help us?"

Kaylia was so excited that she shouted, "Of course we will help you!" not even knowing what they would need to do.

"But, but fairies are not real," said Jack.

"What can we help you with?" asked Kaylia, who was so excited to start helping that she did not even think about her brother and what he wanted.

"We? Uh, no, I think I will just stay here," said Jack. Even though he was older than Kaylia, he was worried and often scared to do anything new.

Kaylia was younger than Jack but braver. She loved to try anything adventurous.

"Oh, come on, you scaredy cat!" argued Kaylia.

"I am not a scaredy cat—you are" Jack responded even though he knew he was lying. Jack was always the scared one, and he knew it, but he did not want anyone else to figure that out.

27

"Prove it," Kaylia demanded, even though she knew that she should probably be more gentle with Jack who was scared, but she also knew that she may never get another chance to see a fairy.

"Stop fighting!" the three older sisters shouted together. (Rosey did not join them because she was still too scared of the humans.)

"We came here for help," Mia explained.

The fairy sisters started to wonder if they had chosen the wrong humans.

Chapter 6
Brought Back a Surprise

As the two human children stood there talking to the four fairy sisters, Jack finally agreed, asking, "Okay, where are we going?"

"We need your help back in our home on Waterfall Island," Makenna told them.

The two humans imagined what it would be like there and thought it sounded magical.

"That is what your home is called?" asked Kaylia, "That is awesome!"

Rosey finally spoke up, inquiring, "What does 'awesome' mean?"

"Never mind, it is just a word that humans say when they think something is great," Kaylia explained.

Hailey began to tell the story of what had happened and how they needed the humans to help them get across the bridge to Crystal Palace where the king and queen lived. The two human children sat quietly the entire time, in shock and unable to believe that they were talking to fairies.

By the end of the story, they were ready to help. "We're in," they said together.

The fairies led the humans back to the portal and started to fly through. Rosey was first this time because she couldn't wait to get back home. One by one the fairies went back through the portal except for Mia who waited to let the humans go first, just to make sure they had not trouble.

Kaylia stepped in front of Jack and started to walk through the portal, but Jack did not want to be left alone, so he grabbed her hand, and they went together.

When Kaylia and Jack went through the portal to Waterfall Island, they thought they were in a dream. There were no houses or streets as they were used to. Instead, they saw green, green grass and beautiful flowers. It looked like a dreamland. The grass was greener than they had ever seen before, and the flowers all around were beautiful.

When Kaylia looked over at the fairies, they were no longer small and tiny in her hand, but instead were just as tall as she was. She thought that as they went through the portal, the fairies must have grown somehow. She looked over at Mia and asked how she had grown so tall.

Mia replied with a smile, "We did not grow tall—you shrunk."

Kaylia looked over to see that Jack had somehow shrunk too, and now they were both the same size as the fairies.

Chapter 7
The Little Things

The quickest way to Crystal Palace was to fly over Mt. Rose, the tallest mountain on Waterfall Island. If they hurried, the fairies knew they could fly there before the sun was at its peak.

There was only one problem—the two humans who had shrunk to fairy size did not have wings. They could not fly.

"How will we get there if Jack and Kaylia can't fly?" sighed Rosey, feeling defeated, "Maybe we should just stay home. Julia might have been wrong."

"There is another way!" shouted Hailey, "There is a tunnel underneath Mt. Rose—it'll be a shortcut. I've seen it on the old maps. It should start just ahead where the river gets closest to the mountain."

None of the fairies had ever been through the tunnel before, and they had no idea what to expect.

They started walking toward the tunnel when they heard something coming from its inside.

"Who goes there?" a creepy voice demanded.

"I think it's coming from inside the tunnel," said Kalia.

"What is it?" Hailey wondered.

"I don't know," Mia announced, "but someone or something is coming! Hide!"

The fairies started to run and hide. Rosey, who had hidden behind the nearest rock as soon as they'd first heard the voice, started to shake.

"Look," whispered Makenna.

"Trolls!" shouted Rosey.

They all started thinking about a way out.

"I guess we will have to make friends," Mia suggested. She had always been the bravest of the fairy sisters. "Who's in?"

Slowly everyone started putting their hand in, including Jack, but Kaylia was nowhere to be found.

"Kaylia, are you coming with us?" whispered Mia, but there was no answer.

"Kaylia! Kaylia!" they all shouted and started to look for her.

"Guys, come look over here," Hailey exclaimed. "The trolls have captured Kaylia!"

Chapter 8
I Can't Believe It!

Once Jack saw his sister surrounded by trolls, much to his own surprise he shouted, "Kaylia, we will save you!" Then he and the fairies started rushing to help her. Jack felt a bit of pride as he ran toward her because he never thought he could say or do something like that in his whole life.

Kaylia, looking over her shoulder, calmly remarked, "Hi guys, come meet Joey . . . Joey, these are my friends."

Kaylia kept speaking, "Joey has a brother named Tommy."

"Nice to meet you all," greeted Tommy.

The fairies stopped in their tracks, in shock.

Jack, very confused, commented, "Trolls are real? First fairies, now trolls? I thought you were kidding when you said they were trolls."

He could not believe his sister had just walked up and started talking to the trolls. Even with his bit of new-found courage, he couldn't imagine having the bravery to just walked up to trolls on his own—the way Kaylia had done.

"Kaylia told us about your journey, and we think we can help," Joey offered.

"That's great!" cried Mia.

"I'm not too sure about this," Makenna commented, "What if it is a trap?"

"Same here," agreed Jack and Rosey at the same time. "We should all stay back."

"Well, I'm gonna go in," protested Mia, "I am not going to give up on finding the crystal."

"I guess we can go, but if we get trapped, it's going to be all on you," noted Makenna.

Tommy exclaimed, "Of course we are not going to trap you—we are friendly. Trolls may look scary and furious, but we are really nice, once you get to know us."

Following the trolls, they started into the dark cave. It was very dark, and they felt dead grass underneath their feet.

Suddenly, it was pitch black and quiet.

Chapter 9
Underneath the Mountain

Nobody but the trolls could see where they were going. Everyone else could only hear footsteps and what sounded like small animals moving in the tunnel. The only way to follow the trolls was by listening to them talk, but their voices started getting softer and softer. Soon the voices were gone, and the fairies and humans stopped.

"Oh no—they walked too far ahead, and we can't see anything!" shouted Makenna.

The group stopped, and they all started to feel cold and afraid. Mia, suddenly remembering her wand, jumped up to remind everyone, "I can make some light with my wand, and we can use it like a lantern."

With a wave of her wand, Mia brought a bright light into the tunnel.

"Oh my!" hollered Kaylia, "I had no idea the tunnel was so big! It's like a giant cave!"

The others looked around and realized that they had walked down into a humungous tunnel that branched into three paths in front of them.

"Oh no! Which path do we take?" asked Rosey.

"Maybe we should split up, and each take a path," Hailey suggested.

"Oh no. I do not want to split up. What if one of the paths leads to monsters?" breathed Jack.

"I agree with Jack," affirmed Rosey, who was also scared, "Let's stay together."

The fairies and humans started talking to each other, louder and louder, trying to come up with a plan, when all of the sudden, they noticed the light from Mia's wand was starting to fade.

"The magic is fading, just like during the ceremony!" cried Makenna.

They all got scared, and the room got quite for a minute.

"Wait—did you hear that?" asked Kaylia, "Everyone—keep quiet."

Listening quietly, as the wand's light finally went out, they heard voices coming from the third tunnel.

"What if it is a group of monsters coming this way to get us?" asked Rosey as she hid behind Mia.

"No wait," whispered Makenna. "It's not a monsters—it's trolls!" she said with excitement.

Straining to hear, she could just make out the voices of Joey and Tommy.

"You were walking too fast, Joey," Tommy complained.

"No, you lost them because you were not paying attention," argued Joey.

The two trolls were arguing so much they almost tripped on the two humans as they came out from the entrance of the third tunnel.

"There you are," said Joey. "See, I told you I would find them!" He looked at Tommy.

"No, I was the one who said to turn around and look, so I found them," cried Tommy.

The fairies were so happy to see the trolls that they didn't even try to stop them from arguing. They just flew up and gave each of them a hug.

During the rest of the journey, the trolls walked more slowly, the humans each held onto the hand of one of the trolls, and the fairies flew so close that they almost bumped into the trolls because nobody wanted to get lost again.

As they traveled through the third tunnel, they saw a bright light in the distance.

51

"We are almost there now," Tommy promised.

"That is the exit, just ahead," Joey told them.

The trolls stopped as tunnel started to open again.

"We are at the end," Tommy said, "but I am afraid we can no longer go with you."

"What? Why not?" asked Mia.

"We cannot go into the sun because it is too bright. But we wish you good luck," Joey told them.

"Can you also give us directions?" asked Makenna.

"Yes," answered Joey, "Just go straight ahead, and there will be a forest. On the other side of the forest will be the castle."

"Thanks a lot, guys!" Kaylia shouted.

"Bye Tommy and Joey," everyone called out.

"Bye everyone," said Tommy and Joey.

Rosey let out a small sigh. She was tired of being in the cave and couldn't wait to fly out in the sky again. As soon as they reached the exit to the cave, she started to fly as high as she could but then froze because she saw someone ahead.

She flew back as quickly as she could to tell the others. She was scared and had a hard time talking. "There is someone up there," she said in a hushed voice, "a fairy dressed in armor, and she looks mean."

The others kept quiet and started to sneak closer to get a better look.

Chapter 10
Who Goes There?

"Should we talk to her?" asked Mia.

"I don't think we should," answered Makenna. "What if she is dangerous?"

As Jack was listening to their conversation, he saw that the girl had a sharp, pointy, stick. "Guys, do you know why she has that stick?" he asked in fear, pointing to what she was holding.

Everyone looked at what Jack was talking about. They all started to worry.

"I don't know," answered Mia.

Suddenly, the girl turned around.

"Who goes there?" she demanded. "You do not have to hide anymore. I know you are there."

Kaylia was scared too, but deciding to face her fear, she spoke up. "We are here," she yelled in a brave voice, "and we are not afraid of you!"

"Show yourselves!" demanded the guardian.

The others did not understand why Kaylia had spoken.

"Why did you just say that?" asked Rosey.

"I did that because I know that if we just hide here, we are never going to see if something is wrong with the Water Crystal," answered Kaylia.

Rosey thought for a moment. At first, she did not like it. Then, she understood the point.

"Okay then," said Rosey.

They all slowly got out of the bushes. When they showed themselves, the guardian asked, "Who are you and why are you here?"

Hailey spoke up first, "Hello, my name is Hailey, and these are my sisters and my friends: Mia, Rosey, Makenna, Jack, and Kaylia. We are here on a journey to Crystal Palace."

"Well, first of all, why did you bring humans? And second of all, why do you want to go to Crystal Palace?" questioned the guardian.

"We want to go to Crystal Palace because we believe that something is wrong with the Water Crystal."

"No fairies except the royal family can cross," barked the guardian, "not even the Guardians of the Crossings can make it over the bridge. That magic is from the King himself and can not be undone."

Jack was confused and spoke up, demanding, "Why do you need to guard the bridge if no one can cross it?"

"The spell keeps all magical creatures from crossing, like fairies, trolls, elves, and even the rarest of all creatures in Waterfall Island, unicorns," replied the guardian, "but every day it is used by animals and creatures without magic."

The bunnies, foxes, birds, and deer bring supplies in and out for the king and queen all the time. It is my job is to make sure no creature is allowed to cross that may harm the king or queen."

"That is why we brought these two," explained Mia pointing to the humans, "because they do not have magic, so they can cross the bridge and speak to the king and queen. We must find out what is going on. There is something wrong with Waterfall Island."

The guardian, starting to lower her stick, told them, "My name is Clara, and I am the guardian of Crystal Palace."

"We were sent by Julia—" started Mia.

"Julia!" Clara interrupted, "If Julia sent you, then of course I will help you."

Mia went on to tell her the story of how their powers were starting to get weaker. Clara agreed to give directions to Crystal Palace and the bridge they must cross to get there.

"How do we start?" questioned Hailey.

"Do you see that tree over there?" asked Clara.

Hailey was confused. There was a bunch of trees, and she did not know which one Clara was talking about. She tried to look where Clara was pointing, but they all looked the same.

"It's the one with a star carved in the trunk. If you look closely, there is a path of trees that all have stars on their trunks. If you follow the path, it will take you to the bridge."

The fairies and humans thanked Clara for her help and then set off to follow the path and find the bridge.

Chapter 11

Crossing the Bridge

As they got closer to the bridge, the air started to get a little colder. Kaylia and Jack noticed that they were walking on glass instead of the grass, and ahead the bridge looked to be made of glass and crystals.

They finally arrived at the bridge.

Mia decided that she would try to fly across it, hoping that maybe the spell was broken, but each time she tried, at the halfway point she flew into a magic barrier. No matter how high she flew the magic barrier was still there.

The fairies looked to Jack and Kaylia, telling them, "You will have to cross to Crystal

Castle on your own. The barrier is too strong for us. It is made from the oldest magic in the land, and the royal family are the only fairies strong enough to disable the barrier."

After taking one last look back at the fairies behind them, Jack and Kaylia started to cross the bridge. Jack was scared that the bridge would fall apart. He closed his eyes lightly.

The bridge felt colder as they moved farther along it. The only thing Kaylia focused on was the crystal. She didn't care if the bridge was cold or not. At the end of the bridge, they saw a gate made out of crystals of all different colors.

Beyond the gate, they saw Crystal Palace. It was one of the most beautiful sights they'd ever even seen. The palace was made completely out of crystals. It had a big doorway outlined in gold.

"Let's go in," insisted Jack, surprising Kaylia, who usually was the one that needed to convince Jack to do anything. She thought to herself that maybe he was starting to get a little braver after all.

As they approached the castle, they felt a cold mist.

Something unique about the bridge and castle was that when anyone touched a railing, wall, or anything made from crystal, suddenly they could remember quite vividly a moment from their past.

Kaylia was the first one to touch a crystal, and she saw Jack running into her room, but he was only three years old, and she was two and a half. The memory—appearing so unexpectedly and seeming so real—frightened her, so she stepped back. As soon as her hand lifted from the crystal, the memory was gone.

"What was that?" she asked in a startled voice.

Jack, just pulling back from another crystal, was shaking. "I just saw my fifth birthday party, it was so real."

"These crystals must be magic. Each one takes you to a different memory of the past."

They decided that it was too much to see all their old memories, so they walked the rest of the way without touching any more crystals.

As they came to the end of the bridge, a fairy man and a fairy woman approached them from inside the castle. They were wearing golden crowns, each with five colored gems, light blue, silver, light green, red, and bright pink.

Kaylia knew at once they must be the king and queen fairy. Kaylia was surprised at how tall they were. They were two times the size of the other fairies they had met.

The queen spoke first, saying, "Hello," in a soft, calm voice.

The king followed and quickly asked, "Who are you and why are you here?"

"Hello, my name is Kaylia, and this my brother, Jack. And we are here to see if something is wrong with the crystals."

The king was surprised. He did not know why they would think something was wrong. But he let them in anyway. He and the queen followed.

Once inside, Kaylia felt warmer.

"Oh no!" cried the queen. "Who would do such a thing?"

Chapter 12

It's a Deal!

The queen was terrified when she entered the grand ballroom.

Jack and Kaylia did not know what to think. They looked at the wall and saw a beautiful sculpture with holding places for five different crystals, but there were only four crystals there.

"Someone has stolen the Water Crystal!" The king was outraged. He did not know what to do. "I am so confused! We have been here the whole time. How could this happen?"

Kaylia stepped forward and told them, "We can help. Jack and I can help you find the crystal and bring it back."

The king ordered, "You must first go back and tell the other fairies that the crystal has been taken. They must do everything they can to get it back! I cannot go because I need to stay here to guard the rest of the crystals. If the Water Crystal is not returned, it could be a disaster for Waterfall Island."

The queen stepped toward Kaylia and Jack, and added, "If you can bring back the Water Crystal, then you will save Waterfall Island. It will not be easy, but if you succeed, then we will make you honorary members of Crystal Kingdom. But hurry, there is not much time."

As they were crossing the bridge back to the fairies, Jack remembered not to touch the crystals because he did not want to be flooded memories.

"We are back, and we have some bad news," Kaylia announced once she reached the four sisters.

The fairies did not like the sound of that, but they needed to hear what was going on.

"Someone has stolen the Water Crystal," continued Jack, "and the king said that if we do not get it back, then it will be a disaster for Waterfall Island."

All as one, the fairies gasped.

Chapter 13

Goodness in the Past,

Evil in the Present

Standing in front of the bridge Hailey spoke up, sharing that she had an idea of who had stolen the crystal, "I think it must be in the evil fairy's treasure vault."

"You mean Floris!" yelled Mia.

All the fairies looked shocked, but the humans did not because they had never heard that name before.

"Who is Floris?" asked Jack.

"Floris is a very evil fairy," explained Rosey. "She steals everyone's most valued treasures and keeps them in her treasure vault."

"And no one has ever been brave enough to go to her palace," continued Makena.

Jack and Kalia couldn't believe there was an evil fairy, because they had assumed all fairies would be nice just like the four sisters.

"Wait a minute," said Mia, "There is no way she could have stolen the crystals. No fairy can cross the bridge—remember!"

"I know," whispered Hailey, "but there is no other fairy in the entire kingdom that would do something like this. She must have found a way."

The group got quiet until Hailey finally spoke up, "I have read the story of how Floris became evil dozens of times in my library at home, and I think that I know how she stole the crystal."

The others looked at Hailey as she told them the story of Floris the evil fairy.

"Floris was not always an evil fairy," Hailey told them, "When she was little, she was kind-hearted and loving."

The fairies and the two human children all sat listening and were eager to hear the rest.

"Her name was not always Floris. She was once known as Felicity. Someone tricked her, and she was heartbroken. She never felt happiness again. It was the saddest day of her life. So she decided that if she was going to be sad, then everyone should be sad."

"But I still don't understand how she was able get across the bridge. You said that no fairy could cross because of a magic spell," exclaimed Kaylia.

"Actually the spell says that no fairy except those in the royal family can cross the bridge, and Floris is the king and queen's daughter!" revealed Hailey.

For the next minute nobody spoke. They were all trying to understand how the daughter of the king and queen, the princess, could turn evil.

Finally Rosey spoke up, "If she has the crystals, then we will never get them back." She moaned as tears started to build up in her eyes. "Her castle is surrounded by a magic wall of thorns that nobody can pass."

Kaylia, looking down at the small fairy who was starting to cover her face, so nobody could see her cry, urged, "There has to be a way. Julia

78

and the king and queen had faith that we could find them, and I do too."

Jack felt bad. He was starting to believe in the fairies, his sister, and himself, and he did not want to give up so soon. He wanted to help more but didn't know how.

"We can't give up now!" he exclaimed, "There has to be a way."

Chapter 14
The Journey to the
Wall of Thorns

The castle of the evil fairy Floris was in the center of Waterfall Island surrounded on all sides by a magic wall that never ended.

"There is only one path to get there," Hailey said. "It goes past stuff that is so dangerous that no fairy has been brave enough to go through it."

"How dangerous can it be?" asked Jack who was starting to feel a bit braver now that he had confronted a troll and been given a quest by a king.

Everyone looked scared, even Mia and Kaylia!

"Okay," they said with fear. "Let's go."

Rosey wanted to show the others that she could be brave too because even Jack was starting to show some courage. Rosey recalled that Julia, the wisest fairy she knew, had told her that she would be the one to save Waterfall Island. But no matter what she tried, Rosey couldn't help but feel afraid of what was down the path.

At the start of the path, much to Rosey's relief, there was nothing that seemed dangerous. Even though it looked as if no fairy had been that way in years, the start of the path appeared just as bright and colorful as the rest of Waterfall Island. But as they got farther down the path, it began to get more scary. It was dark, the wind was howling, and it was very cold.

Suddenly, Mia stopped. "What was that sound?" she asked.

"I'm not sure, but I can tell it is not good," Makenna remarked.

G-R-R-R-R-R-R-R-OWL!

"Wolves! Fly!" shouted Rosey.

Immediately the fairies started to fly while the humans could only run. The wolves chased the brother and sister until they reached a dead-end. The wolves, seeing that the humans were trapped, started to slowly walk back and forth in front of them, getting ready to pounce. The largest of the wolves went first, pointing itself toward Kaylia and preparing to leap.

Rosey saw what was happening and wanted to do something, anything, to help. But she froze, and all could do was scream, "Watch out!"

The other fairies quickly turned and saw the danger. Makenna acted before anyone else could even think. She flew down right in front of the wolf just as it was getting ready to pounce.

At first the wolf just snarled its teeth at the young fairy, but soon its face started to change. The snarl turned into a grin, and the wolf sat down. Makenna pointed her wand back down the trail where they had come from and the wolf slowly got up ad walked off. The other wolves followed, and soon the four fairies and the two human children were alone again.

"Whew! That was a close one!" cried Hailey. "How did you do that?"

"I am not sure," whispered Makenna, "I've always been able to help animals, but I never knew I could do something like that. I used all the magic I could, and somehow it worked. I told them not to harm us."

The rest, too tired to hear them, were catching their breath. It all seemed like a dream to them—a bad dream—but it wasn't. As they looked around, they realized that while the wolves had been chasing them, they had lost the path.

Rosey groaned, "I can't believe it! We are lost in the forest and will never get to the Wall of Thorns now."

At that, Mia had an idea. She flew up as high as she could above the forest. She looked in all directions, hoping she was close enough to see the Wall of Thorns. She saw a long wall of branches at the edge of the forest, but she could not tell if it was really the Wall of Thorns.

After deciding it was worth a try, Mia flew down to the others and guided them through the forest to the place she'd seen from above.

As soon as they made it through the forest, Kaylia stopped. "Whoa!" she cried, "Look—the Wall of Thorns!"

They all looked ahead of them.

That was it, the wall that surrounded the castle that Floris now used as her evil lair.

But it was no ordinary wall. It was made up of the stems of rose bushes thick with thorns. Floris had long ago cursed it with a powerful magic, and no matter how high or far the fairies tried to fly over or around it, the wall just kept going.

Then they heard something.

"Guys! Quick! It's Floris!" Hailey yelled.

 86

"Everyone be calm—but also hide," commanded Mia. Quietly and quickly, they all hid.

"Well, on the bright side, we might be able to see how she gets through," noted Jack. "We just need to send someone to go watch her, and then, we will do the same thing she did."

"I'm not doing it!" shouted Rosey.

"Who will do it?" asked Makenna.

It grew very, very, quiet for a couple of seconds.

"I will do it," answered Mia.

They all wished Mia good luck. Then Mia set off.

As Mia watched Floris, she felt afraid. "What if she sees me? Will she cast a spell on me?" Mia wondered.

Suddenly, Floris looked behind her—in Mia's direction. Without a moment to spare, Mia hid behind the bushes.

Floris moved to a spot in the wall that had a black stick that was different from the rest. She did a magic spell that made a secret door appear out of nowhere. Then Floris walked in—effortlessly.

Chapter 15
Of Course, Magic

"So that's how she goes through—magic!" Mia cheered quietly.

She went to tell the others. "I found out how she does it!"

"How?" Jack asked.

"She uses a magic spell," answered Mia.

The fairies all looked at Mia, declaring, "We should have known."

"Let me show you—" guided Mia.

Then all of the sudden, the ground started shaking.

Jack shouted, "What was that?"

91

Rosey hid behind Mia, her wings starting to fold down in fear.

Mia replied, "I don't know for sure, but even I am afraid to find out. We better hurry."

The fairies all flew back to the Wall of Thorns as fast as they could. Jack and Kaylia ran to catch up. When they reached the wall, Mia showed them the branch that was darker than the rest, a pure black in the middle of all the green and brown.

It had thorns that were a different color than all the rest.

Kaylia and Jack started to say, "Alakazam! . . . Open sesame."

Mia looked at them and laughed, "Oh, silly humans, that is not how it works. You need to use a magic wand, and there are no funny words."

Mia tapped three times on the leaf with her wand, then made a circle around the branch, and tapped one more time. The branch that was pure black turned rainbow-colored, and a secret door opened.

The four fairies and the two humans gathered their courage and stepped inside.

Chapter 16
Inside the Wall of Thorns

"Whoa! It is so dark in here!" yelled Hailey.

"And really scary!" cried Kaylia.

"Guys, there's Floris! Right there!" Hailey shrieked in horror.

Still frightened, they looked ahead to see Floris casting a spell to make a throne out of pixie dust. Then, she started to laugh, and the pixie dust faded away.

Since it was mostly dark, Floris did not see the group of fairies and humans sneaking in.

"Pretty soon the kingdom will be mine!" Floris screeched.

The Water Crystal too was in the dark room, placed on a table surrounded by pills, potions, and books with magic spells. They were all labeled with names like Panic Potion, Laugh Attack Potion, or Book of Black Roses. The Water Crystal sat in a glass case upon a little table that was levitating and covered in a red cloth. The crystal was shining its brightest light.

Floris paused for a moment, as if she were considering something or looking for something. Then she left the area, going out the back.

"This is our chance to get the crystal, guys!" cried Mia. "While Floris is out, we can get the crystal!"

The fairies flew up to grab the crystal, all except Rosey who stayed back because she was too scared to move. She wanted to go, but inside she felt afraid so much that her wings would not move. The two humans stayed back and watched because they could not fly.

Just as the three fairy sisters got closer to the crystal on the flying table, Floris returned with some items in her hands. At first, Floris did not notice them. But after setting down the items, she saw the three fairies and immediately looked very red and angry. Floris quickly took out her wand. It was very shiny and black, similar to the special branch in the Wall of Thorns. Floris then positioned her wand as if she were about to cast a spell.

"Wait!" shouted Kaylia.

Upon hearing this word, Floris quickly turned around and was about to freeze Kaylia too, but instead Floris paused to ask, "Where are your wings?"

Silence fell into the room.

Kaylia knew that she couldn't let Floris know that she was a human.

When Floris turned back around, she just caught sight of the three fairies grabbing the Water Crystal.

"Oh no you don't!" yelled Floris, magically freezing the three fairies. Then she turned her attention back to Kaylia—and froze her too!

"You're too late anyway," Floris remarked, "Do you feel the ground shaking? If the crystal stays away from Crystal Palace for more than twenty-four hours, then Waterfall Island will start to move away from the other islands and Crystal Palace for good. Soon the bridge will break, and there will be no way to get back to

Crystal Palace. I will have the crystal all to myself, and I will start my own kingdom. Soon you will all bow to me as queen!"

Chapter 17
Defeated

Rosey was scared but knew she had to do something. She had to make a decision on whether she was going to help or keep hiding.

She finally made a decision—to help her sisters and Kaylia.

"Jack, I need your help," she said. Jack was surprised at seeing Rosey so brave!

"Okay, what is it?" he questioned.

"I need you to distract Floris. Then, I will grab her wand, unfreeze your sister and my sisters, and get the crystal back. Okay?" asked Rosey.

Jack nodded in agreement but was not sure that he could actually do it.

Jack stood up straight and began to do his part of the plan while Rosey did her part of it.

Jack thought, "Since I am small, Floris will not see me, so I can lift up her potions, and she will not know what is happening."

He looked to the shelf of potions above where Floris was standing and saw one labeled "Laugh Attack." Then he thought, "I can lift up the laughing potion and spill it on her, and she will not be able to stop laughing." He started to do his plan.

He climbed up, lifted the bottle of laughing potion, and spilled it on Floris. Immediately Floris was not able to stop laughing.

While Jack was busy distracting Floris, Rosey flew up to Floris's black and purple dress, and quickly grabbed her wand.

"Got it," she thought. Then Rosey waved the wand in the air and froze Floris so that she could not move. Floris's face was cemented in a funny expression too.

After she'd frozen Floris, Rosey unfroze her sisters and Kaylia.

"Wow! I'm very surprised!" exclaimed Mia. "You're very brave."

"Yes—thank you. You are right—I was brave, but also I had to do it," Rosey replied with a bright smile. She had finally done it. She had shown the others that she too could be brave, and she had proved to herself that could save Waterfall Island.

Kaylia turned to Jack, who had just finished climbing down from the table, and hugged him tightly. "You did it Jack, you saved the day!"

Jack felt bright inside. Before this magical trip, he had never felt brave, but now he knew that he could do anything and would never be scaredy cat ever again.

Then, Makenna remembered something. She flew up and grabbed the crystal. "Guys! I have it!" she hollered and quickly flew back down.

"That's great!" Jack said.

"Now let's get out of here before Floris catches us!" said Makenna.

"Oh, I have already dealt with that," Rosey replied. "Now let's get out of here!"

As they left the Wall of Thorns, the ground started shaking. They all knew it was because the crystal was gone from Crystal Palace and Waterfall Island was starting to separate from the rest of the Crystal Kingdom.

They started to walk faster and faster as the ground started shaking more and more.

"Hurry," Mia warned, "We must get back to Crystal Palace before it's too late!"

Chapter 18

Saying Good-bye (I Think)

The journey back through the forest was less creepy and scary now that they knew the way. The wolves had been scared into their homes from the ground shaking and did not bother them. The humans ran as fast as they could with the fairies right beside them.

When they saw the bridge still intact, their hearts lifted.

"We are gonna make it," declared Rosey, who was still so excited and felt a new change inside her. She was no longer scared.

As the two humans began crossing the bridge, the ground started shaking again. When they finished crossing it, the ground was shaking so hard that it broke the bridge.

"Oh no!" cried Kaylia. "The bridge broke! We might not ever see the fairies again!"

"I guess this is good-bye," murmured Kaylia, looking back toward the fairies and waving as tears filled her beautiful, little eyes.

"How are we going to get home?" Jack asked.

Feeling defeated, they turned towards the castle and went in. The door shut, and they thought that they would never see their fairy friends again.

Chapter 19
Solve the Puzzle

As they were entering the castle, Jack and Kaylia noticed that it had changed. All the beautiful memory crystals were starting to fade.

The king and queen were in the ballroom waiting when Jack and Kaylia burst through the door.

"We found the crystal!" they announced.

"We know, and we are so proud of you!" the king and queen responded.

The humans froze.

"Wait, how did you know that we found it?" asked Kaylia.

"We have been watching your journey in our crystal ball," the king shared.

"And you have done an excellent job!" added the queen.

The ground started shaking again, this time more violently than ever before. The castle started cracking.

The queen urged, "We have to hurry and put the Water Crystal back before the island breaks away. Once the crystal is back in place, Waterfall Island will regain all of its power."

"Okay, let's put the crystal back before it is too late," Kaylia agreed.

They quickly put the crystal in its special holding place.

Once the crystal was back in its position, the ground stopped shaking. The bridge magically came together again. And once Jack and Kaylia saw the bridge come back together, they ran to see their fairy friends!

"Guys," they said, "we thought we would never see you again!"

"We did too!" the fairies shouted in reply.

They all hugged each other and celebrated.

The king and queen walked across the bridge to meet the fairies. The fairies were so excited. It was not every day that they got to meet the king and queen of the Crystal Kingdom. They all squealed with joy. The king congratulated each of the fairies and saved a special moment for Rosey and Jack.

"Rosey and Jack," he declared, "your combined bravery has saved everyone on Waterfall Island."

Rosey and Jack were both speechless. They each were happy to no longer feel scared and they wanted to keep it that way.

Then the king turned to include Kaylia too. To Jack and Kaylia, the king stated, "You have proven that you are capable of great things, and from now on, I am making you official members of the Crystal Kingdom. You may come visit anytime, as long as you keep our kingdom a secret."

He then gave them a locket with pixie dust inside.

"Whenever you want to return, you can go back to the magic tree that brought you here, sprinkle the pixie dust on it, and return through its portal," explained the king.

Chapter 20

Back Home

A few hours later, the fairies were back home and practicing their water dancing skills. Jack and Kaylia were with them and eager to watch them dance. Now that the Water Crystal was back in place, the Crystal Ceremony could start again.

Jack and Kaylia watched in wonder as the fairies danced on the pond and fireworks lit the sky.

After the ceremony the humans went back to their home, and so did the fairies.

"Do you think that we will ever see Jack and Kaylia again?" asked Rosey.

Mia laughed and replied, "I don't know, but if we do, I am sure that it will be magical!"

THE END

About the Author

At 8 years old, Emma Sumner is one of the youngest authors to write a fairytale book. She loves the *Rainbow Magic* books by Daisy Meadows and *The Never Girls Collection* by Disney, and cannot wait to see her own book on the bookshelf next to them.

Emma lives in Northern California and is getting ready to go into the third grade. When she is not reading or writing, she spends most of her time playing outside with her friends and family, dancing Hula, or practicing gymnastics.

Her dream is to become an author and to continue the adventures of *The Fairies of Waterfall Island* into a series.

To find out more about Emma and *The Fairies* *of* *Waterfall* *Island* go to www.EmmaLovesBooks.com

53720019R00074

Made in the USA
San Bernardino, CA
26 September 2017